Melissa's Halloween Wish

BY DONA ROSS PRATT

Illustrated by Megan Cunningham

Little Creek Press
A Division of Kristin Mitchell Design, LLC
5341 Sunny Ridge Road
Mineral Point, Wisconsin 53565

Limited First Edition
October 2012

Printed in Wisconsin, United States of America.

For more information or to order books:
www.littlecreekpress.com

Library of Congress Control Number: 2012948452

ISBN-10: 0984924574
ISBN-13: 978-0-9849245-7-8

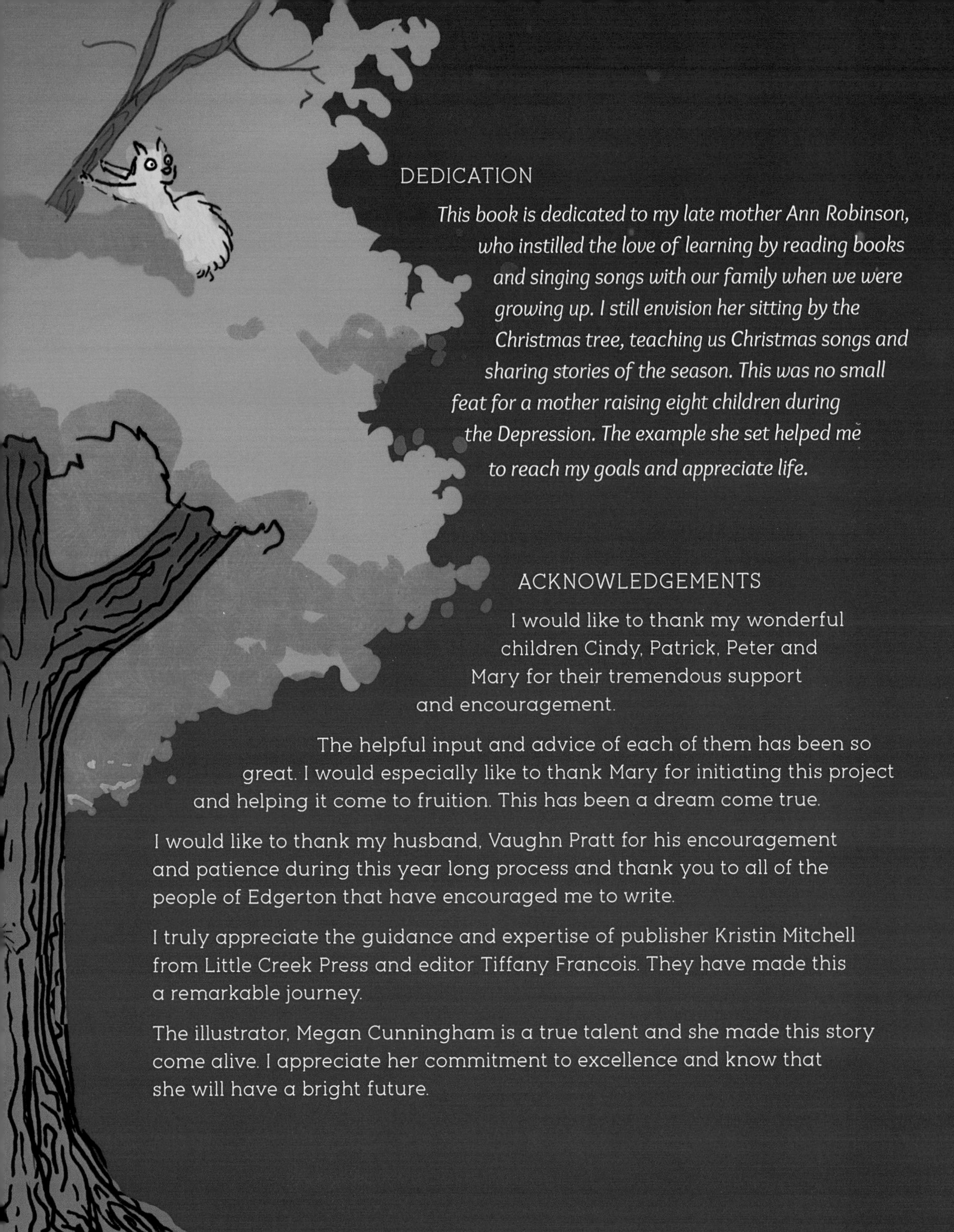

DEDICATION

This book is dedicated to my late mother Ann Robinson, who instilled the love of learning by reading books and singing songs with our family when we were growing up. I still envision her sitting by the Christmas tree, teaching us Christmas songs and sharing stories of the season. This was no small feat for a mother raising eight children during the Depression. The example she set helped me to reach my goals and appreciate life.

ACKNOWLEDGEMENTS

I would like to thank my wonderful children Cindy, Patrick, Peter and Mary for their tremendous support and encouragement.

The helpful input and advice of each of them has been so great. I would especially like to thank Mary for initiating this project and helping it come to fruition. This has been a dream come true.

I would like to thank my husband, Vaughn Pratt for his encouragement and patience during this year long process and thank you to all of the people of Edgerton that have encouraged me to write.

I truly appreciate the guidance and expertise of publisher Kristin Mitchell from Little Creek Press and editor Tiffany Francois. They have made this a remarkable journey.

The illustrator, Megan Cunningham is a true talent and she made this story come alive. I appreciate her commitment to excellence and know that she will have a bright future.

Melissa turned and waved goodbye to her mother as she started up the path with her new shiny broom. She was on her way to "Miss Trindell's School for Witches." At the big oak tree, she met her best friend, Meghan, who wasn't a witch. Melissa told the most fanciful stories about Halloween and Meghan loved to listen to them.

"Oh Meghan, I am so excited! It is Halloween and I will take my first solo broom ride!" exclaimed Melissa. "I sure hope I can remember everything!"

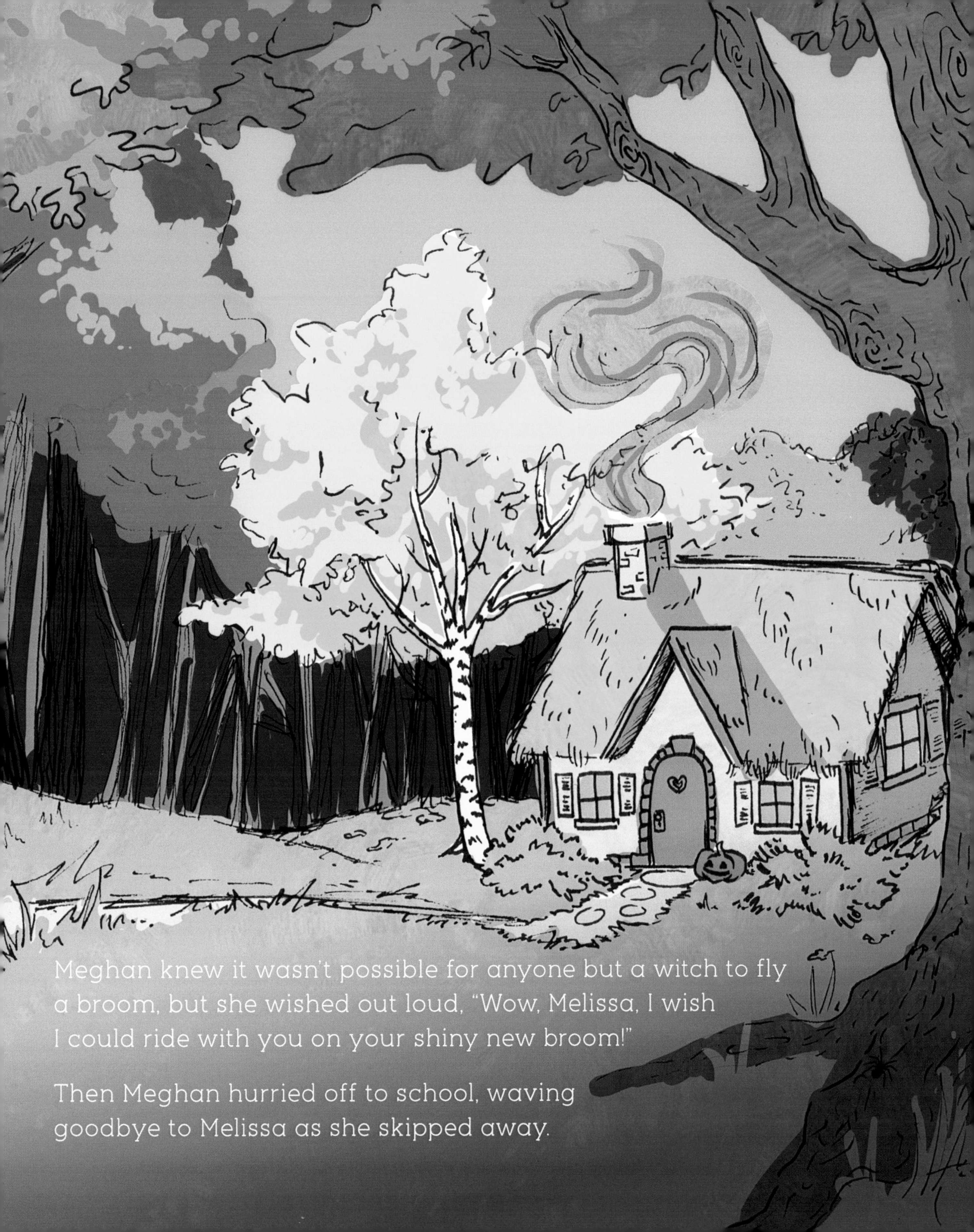

Meghan knew it wasn't possible for anyone but a witch to fly a broom, but she wished out loud, "Wow, Melissa, I wish I could ride with you on your shiny new broom!"

Then Meghan hurried off to school, waving goodbye to Melissa as she skipped away.

Melissa

At school Melissa took her seat with the other excited little witches. When class started Miss Trindell led all the little witches in their daily song.

"A special witch is what I'll be; wait and see; wait and see; there will never be a better witch, than the likes of me!"

When they finished singing, Miss Trindell opened "The Big Book of Magic Tricks." She turned to the page with their favorite magic trick, "How to Disappear." The little witches had been practicing this trick since their very first day. Then, before Miss Trindell could count one, two, three, there wasn't a little witch left to see!

The witches reappeared quickly and Miss Trindell called on Melissa to demonstrate flying with her broom. Melissa grabbed her broom, took a deep breath, and repeated the magic words,

"Abba, shabba, wabba, woo, dibble, dabble, rabble, roo."

Melissa slowly flew forward and backward, up high and down low, and gently landed back on her feet.
All the witches clapped in delight.

SPELLS

Miss Trindell gathered the excited new witches in the forest. "Now it's time for all of you to help me mix the magic Halloween brew for tonight." The girls crowded around the pot as she chanted,

"Take a tadpole tail and a black cat's hair. Stir it round and round till it comes out clear. Add three leaves from the hemlock tree, and the magic powder of witches' tea."

Puff! Puff! Wham! Colors swirled and popped as each little witch poured in the powders and took turns mixing the magic brew.

"Now," said Miss Trindell, "I have a surprise for you!"
The little witches listened very carefully as she spoke,

"Deep in the woods is a golden box, behind a door, with a golden lock. The first little witch to find this treasure, may wish a wish to give her pleasure. If the moon is shining with golden light, her wish will be granted this very night!"

Miss Trindell grew very serious. She cautioned the little witches, "I must warn you. Beware of Grumpy Gretchen Witch. With a big black cat on her broom, she frightens new little witches and will try to find the treasure before you do."

The little witches hurried home to get ready for the magical night. When they returned they gathered around the pot of magic brew and sang:

"A special witch is what I'll be; wait and see; wait and see; there will never be a better witch; than the likes of me!"

Miss Trindell gave the witches last minute instructions and warned them again about Grumpy Gretchen Witch. Jumping on their brooms, the little witches repeated the magic words,

"Abba, shabba; wabba, woo; dibble, dabble; rabble, roo."

Up and up and up they flew. Melissa zoomed from cloud to cloud and over the forest. The little witches soared about looking for the secret treasure.

The moon was shining brightly and Melissa was gliding happily. Suddenly, something large and black zoomed out from behind a cloud. It was a witch with a big black cat on her broom!

"It's Grumpy Gretchen! What shall I do?" thought Melissa. Remembering the most important trick, she quickly disappeared. When she reappeared, there was Grumpy Gretchen swooping down at her.

"Go away! Leave me alone!" yelled Melissa. Grumpy Gretchen zoomed closer to Melissa.

"Well, well, what do we have here!" screeched Grumpy Gretchen.

Melissa was so frightened that she lost her balance and tumbled down, down, down! Crash! She landed in a tree. Her skirt was tangled and caught so that Melissa could not get free!

"I'll never find the treasure now," sighed Melissa. Then she heard a strange sound and out from a hole in the tree popped Ollie Owl. He was the largest owl Melissa had ever seen.

"Whoo-oo-oo's out here? Whoooo are you?" asked Ollie Owl.

"I'm a little witch. I've fallen out of the sky and am stuck in this tree. Could you please help me?" asked Melissa.

"Of course, I'll help you-oooo," said Ollie Owl. He untangled Melissa from the branches and helped her to the ground.

"Thank you, Ollie Owl. Now I can search for the treasure," Melissa said.

“What is that? Treasure you say? I have been waiting all year for this moment,” said Ollie Owl with great big glowing eyes. He pushed some branches aside with his large wing and revealed a small door with a golden lock. Reaching into his feathers, Ollie Owl pulled out a key and opened the door.

Inside was a shiny golden box.

“The treasure! It’s the treasure!” exclaimed Melissa. As she touched the golden box, it flew open and inside was a dazzling wish charm.

Suddenly, Grumpy Gretchen reappeared! She swooped down, grabbed the bright wish charm and up and away she flew!

"Oh no," screamed Melissa. "Come back! That's MY treasure, you greedy, graspy, old witch!"

Grumpy Gretchen bolted off chanting,

"Snickerty Snackerty; crim, crum, crackerty; alakazim and alakazime; now that I have it; the treasure is mine."

Snappy Squirrel, who lived up in the tree, saw what happened and scrambled down to see how he could help. Melissa pulled out her magic wand, pointed it at Snappy Squirrel, and recited a magic spell,

"Hither, dither; scurry, scurry; spread the word; hurry, hurry!

Poof! The spell shot Snappy Squirrel to the very top of the tallest tree. He chattered out an emergency signal that alerted all the squirrels in the woods. From tree to tree the message traveled, "Find Grumpy Gretchen, she has stolen the treasure!"

The squirrels took off in search of Grumpy Gretchen. "She's there!" one of the squirrels chattered, "behind that big tree!"

Melissa waved her wand over the squirrels and chanted,

"Zimba, zoomba; zappity, zap; squirrels become the magic trap!"

At once, all the squirrels surrounded her before she could fly away.

Melissa raced in to gather up Grumpy Gretchen's magic hat, wand, and the wish charm. Grumpy Gretchen and her mean magic were powerless and the good little witches were free of her at last!

Melissa thanked Ollie Owl and Snappy Squirrel. Waving goodbye, she flew up and away to show Miss Trindell the wish charm.

Miss Trindell clapped her hands in excitement! She took the wish charm from Melissa and said, “As the moon is shining with a golden light, your wish will be granted this very night!”

Melissa spun around, whirling up in the air on her broom. “I wish, I wish,” said Melissa, “for my good friend Meghan to ride with me on my broom tonight!”

Melissa zipped off to Meghan's house. She scooped up Meghan on her broom and said the magic words,

"Abba, shabba; wabba, woo: dibble, dabble; rabble, roo."

Away they flew. They zoomed up past the moon and down, nearly touching the ground! "Oh Melissa," Meghan said, "let's ride over the whole town!"

They were soon looking down over their little town. The lights were shining brightly and the streets were filled with boys and girls dressed in costumes of every shape and color. They were busy trick or treating and dashing from house to house. “Oh Melissa, this night is like a wonderful dream,” said Meghan.

After gliding, soaring, and speeding through the night sky, Melissa said, “It’s time for me to take you home now, Meghan.”

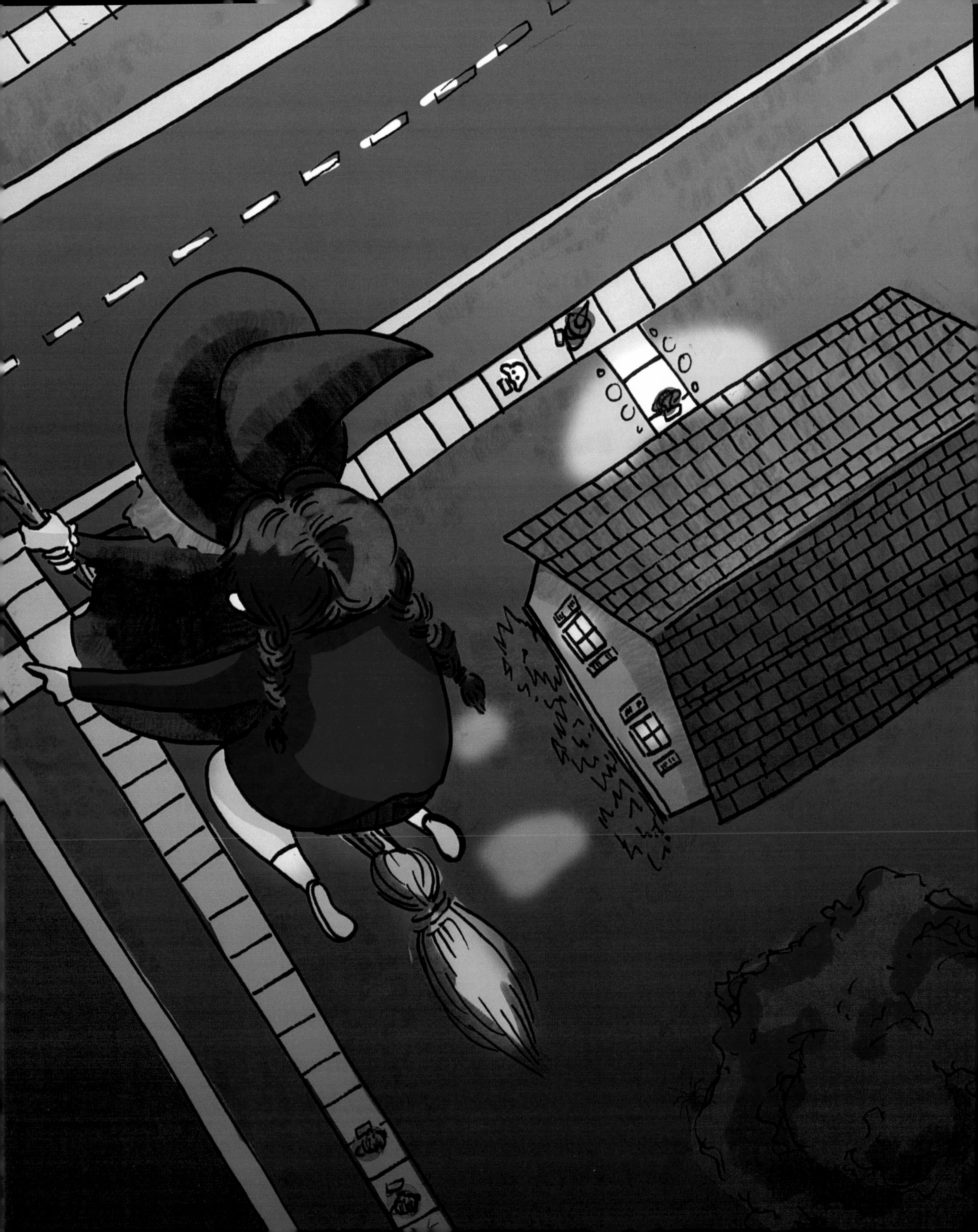

HAPPY HALLOW

When they reached Meghan's house they looked down and saw all of their friends and family. "It's a party!" said Melissa. There in Meghan's backyard was a big banner with the words, HAPPY HALLOWEEN!

When they landed on the ground everyone gathered to greet them. They all cheered and celebrated with Halloween goodies. It was a wonderful Halloween night and a magical Halloween ride.

Miss Trindell's School For Witches Daily Song

By Dona Ross Pratt

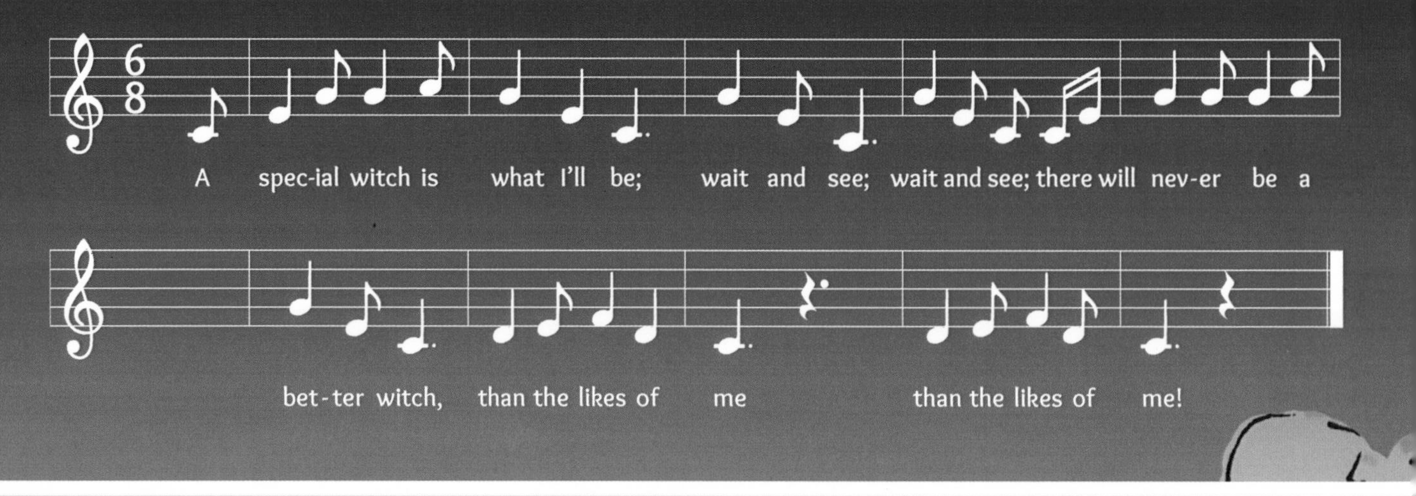

About the Author

Dona Ross Pratt grew up in Brodhead, Wisconsin in a family of eight children. Upon her graduation from Brodhead High School she furthered her education at the Whitewater State Teachers College. She graduated with a degree in kindergarten and primary education. She taught in Columbus, Beloit and Fox Point, Wisconsin before moving to Edgerton, where she and her husband Dr. Francis Ross, raised their family of four children.

Her true commitment was to family and for years she maintained her love of teaching by being a substitute teacher in the School District of Edgerton. In 1984 Dona decided to open a creative arts preschool that she managed and taught in for fifteen years. She thoroughly enjoyed watching children develop a love of learning, along with creatively expressing themselves through art and music. It was during this time she was inspired to begin writing this book.

She has been an avid lover of children's literature for years and spent countless hours reading books to children in school, her own children at home and her grandchildren. She feels that reading books fosters children's imaginations and helps inspire them to learn.

About the Illustrator

Megan Cunningham is an aspiring author/illustrator currently working towards her Bachelor's Degree of Fine Arts at the Milwaukee Institute of Art and Design. She has always had a strong affinity for both art and a good story, and loves being able to bring the two together. Her favorite part of illustrating is creating a rich and layered experience for each reader. "Melissa's Secret Wish" is Megan's debut into the professional illustration world.